To: Stirling
Smiles ❤!
Mama Judy

MW01273825

CalviN caN...
...bE aNGRy

judy EdwaRd

Produced by:

FriesenPress

Suite 300 – 852 Fort Street
Victoria, BC, Canada V8W 1H8

www.friesenpress.com

Distributed to the trade by The Ingram Book Company

Once upon a time
In a land far, far away
Where anything was possible. . .
There lived a boy named Calvin.

Calvin was not having a good day.

When he woke up in the morning
it was still dark.

Mommy and Daddy did not
want to play so early.

They sent him back to his room.

When he went back to his bedroom to play by himself he stepped on his fire truck and hurt his big toe.

Calvin decided to get dressed
all by himself.

He put on his favorite shorts.

When Mommy saw him in his shorts she said "You can't wear shorts today Calvin. It's too cold outside. You must put on your warm pants."

"NO!" shouted Calvin.

"I want to wear my shorts."

He stamped his foot and made an angry face.

Daddy said "Put some warm pants on right now. We must go to work and you must go to your grandmother's house. You can choose your grey pants or your blue jeans, but you must hurry up!"

Calvin chose his grey pants.
He hurried to the car, but he was
still angry on the inside.

When Calvin got to his "Mama's" house he decided to play with his blocks.

He tried to make a truck, but the wheels would not stay on.

The more Calvin tried to make the wheels stay on, the more upset he became.

Finally Calvin threw the wheels across the room and shouted, "AAUGH! These blocks make me SO angry!"

Mama came running into the room.

"Calvin, why are you shouting?
What is wrong?"

"I HATE these blocks!" yelled Calvin and he threw another handful of blocks on the floor.

"Calvin!" said Mama in a stern voice. "You must stop yelling and throwing your blocks."

"BUT I AM ANGRY!" yelled Calvin.

"I can see that you are angry."
said Mama.

"Let's walk away from these blocks.

Let's walk around the house for a few
minutes until you feel less angry."

Calvin walked with Mama and he did feel a little better, but he was still angry.

"How do you feel now?" asked Mama.

"I am still angry." said Calvin.

"Do you still feel like throwing your blocks?" asked Mama.

Yes I do!" said Calvin loudly.

"Let's think about that." said Mama.

"What will happen if you throw
your blocks?"

"They could break." said Calvin.
"They could break my other toys.
They could hurt someone."

"Let's find something else to do with your angry feelings instead of throwing blocks." said Mama.

Mama went into her closet and came out with a big soft pillow.

"What can we do with this?"
she asked.

Calvin shook the pillow.

Calvin yelled into the pillow.

Calvin jumped on the pillow.

Nothing was hurt or broken...

And . . . Calvin felt better.

"How do you feel now?" asked Mama.

"I feel just a little bit angry."
said Calvin.

"Then let's color the last of your
angry feelings away." said Mama.

Mama gave Calvin an angry face and some crayons.

Calvin colored his angry face.

Then he tore it up and threw it away.

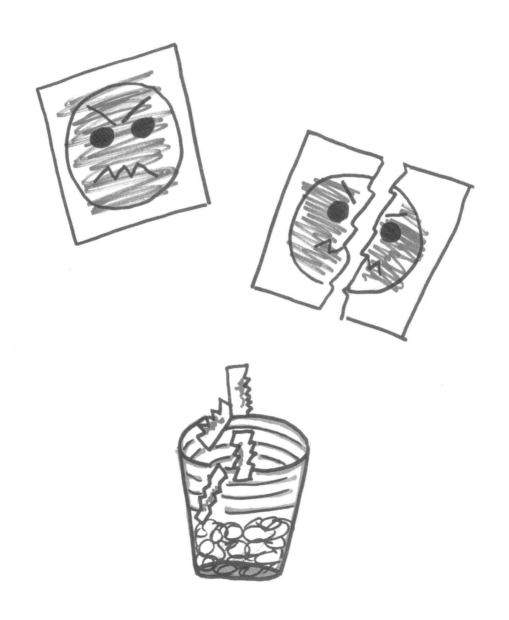

Mama gave him another face to color.
This one was a happy face.

"Let's think about all the things that
make you happy while you color."
said Mama.

Calvin thought hard.
Then he began to smile.

Calvin colored his
happy face and put
it on the fridge.

"Who can work out his angry feelings?" asked Mama.

"Calvin can!" shouted Calvin.

"Everyone can." smiled Mama.

Calvin's Angry Face

Calvin's Sad Face

Calvin's Happy Face

The lesson of this book is an incredibly valuable one that both children (and, or perhaps especially, their adult caregivers!) will greatly benefit from. The story isn't about Calvin learning that being angry isn't o.k. – rather, he learns that he can move through the emotion and into a more peaceful state without resorting to or relying on aggression to do so. Mama helps Calvin understand the potential consequences of acts done in anger by encouraging him to think for himself about what might happen, not by scolding and lecturing him. This is a teachable moment in non-escalation (for caregivers) as well as in independent thought (for kids).

Sarah Stewart, Editor, Children's books

Judy Edward is the wise grandmother every child should have. As she did with the first book in the series, Calvin Can Be Happy, she wraps young Calvin in loving acceptance and makes it safe for him to work through his emotions. This time it is that fierce demon we all hold inside and that explodes as anger. Mama helps Calvin re-route his angry feelings in a way that makes him feel heard and understood. Everyone who loves a child or works with them in any setting will want this book, to share over and over.

Cathryn Wellner, Professional Storyteller
School Librarian (retired),
Blogger: Catching Courage, Crossroads, StoryRoute
This Gives Me Hope

CPSIA information can be obtained
at www.ICGtesting.com
Printed in the USA
LVIC06n0546280114
371171LV00001BA/1